Once Upon A Dream

Verses Of Wonder

Edited By Lynsey Evans

First published in Great Britain in 2024 by:

YoungWriters
Est. 1991

Young Writers
Remus House
Coltsfoot Drive
Peterborough
PE2 9BF
Telephone: 01733 890066
Website: www.youngwriters.co.uk

All Rights Reserved
Book Design by Ashley Janson
© Copyright Contributors 2024
Softback ISBN 978-1-83565-431-6
Printed and bound in the UK by BookPrintingUK
Website: www.bookprintinguk.com
YB0590T

FOREWORD

Welcome Reader, to a world of dreams.

For Young Writers' latest competition, we asked our writers to dig deep into their imagination and create a poem that paints a picture of what they dream of, whether it's a make-believe world full of wonder or their aspirations for the future.

The result is this collection of fantastic poetic verse that covers a whole host of different topics. Let your mind fly away with the fairies to explore the sweet joy of candy lands, join in with a game of fantasy football, or you may even catch a glimpse of a unicorn or another mythical creature. Beware though, because even dreamland has dark corners, so you may turn a page and walk into a nightmare!

Whereas the majority of our writers chose to stick to a free verse style, others gave themselves the challenge of other techniques such as acrostics and rhyming couplets.

Each piece in this collection shows the writers' dedication and imagination – we truly believe that seeing their work in print gives them a well-deserved boost of pride, and inspires them to keep writing, so we hope to see more of their work in the future!

CONTENTS

Bridgwater College Academy, Bridgwater

Tamzin Buller (10)	1
Erin McCallum (8)	2
Emilis Kisel (11)	4
Olivia Aldridge (9)	5
Jessica Wilkin (7)	6
Amelia Bowers (10)	7
Abigail Palasti (10)	8
Lily-May Stockham (9)	9
Nara Leigh Black (8)	10
Indie Tottle (9)	11
Izabella Clarke (11)	12
Alice Walford (8)	13
Lacey-Rose Peploe (10)	14
Scarlett Finn (10)	15

Brightwell cum Sotwell CE Primary School, Brightwell cum Sotwell

Emma Richards (10)	16
Ariel To (10)	17
Ziva Osman (10)	18
Maeve Norfolk (10)	19
Abbie Prior (10)	20
Allegra Benarr (10)	21
Molly Horrocks (10)	22
Maggie Horrocks (10)	23
Molly Smith de Brito (10)	24
Molly Brack (9)	25

Greenleaf Primary School, London

Aminah Majid (9)	26
Anam Husain (10)	27
Inaya Dhami (9)	28
Sophia Ellin (10)	29

Larchfield Primary & Nursery School, Maidenhead

Veerangana Saraiya (10)	30
Hannah Carvalho (9)	32
Kenza Olarewaju (9)	33

Manea Community Primary School, Manea

Louis Garner (11)	34
Ronnie Richardson (8)	35
Violet Ronald (8)	36
Abbey Proctor (9)	38
Lorna Garlick (11)	39
Evie Marshall (10)	40
Maisie Law (10)	41
Charlie Harding (10)	42
Clara Bembridge (9)	43
Molly Grannell (10)	44
Raine Wilkes (10)	45
Melody Millward (11)	46
Sienna Scarff (10)	47
Noah Evans (9)	48
Emily Swinden (10)	49
Lydia Lane (11)	50
Izi Barnes-Stubbins (9)	51
Theodore Kerans (11)	52

Harley Young (8)	53
Lily O'Reilly (10)	54
Josie McKew (9)	55
Alice Bembridge (11)	56
Jack Turner (11)	57
Mia Stock (10)	58
Mia Scarff (10)	59
Oliver McGee (8)	60
Roman Boyce (9)	61
Aryanna Scarff (8)	62
Dennis Dean (8)	63
Georgia Polley (10)	64
Charlie Fyson (11)	65
Elliot Skeggs (10)	66
Harris Farrer (7)	67
Alfie Youfens (11)	68
Darcy Bradford (8)	69
Ronnie Hassall (7)	70
Poppy Smith (11)	71
Rowan Clegg (7)	72
Charlie Newsmith (8)	73
Leon Garner (7)	74
Isaac Beeken (10)	75
Archie Ronald (10)	76
Oscar Ash (7)	77
Abby Calder (10)	78
Jimmy Eric Dean Lane (9)	79
Ivy Tasker (7)	80
Emra Day (10)	81
Mason Lemmon (10)	82
Jenson Day (9)	83
Farys Thompson (8)	84
Josh Skeggs (8)	85
Imogen Lakin (8)	86
Ella Harrison (8)	87
Jake Lee (10)	88
Tyler Shadbolt (10)	89
Jesse Markowski (7)	90
Kayden-Jack Barnes (7)	91
Taylor Judd (11)	92
Charlie Doggett (8)	93
Jacob Drummond (8), Noah Kendall (7) & Tarley Brown (7)	94
Ralph Daniel (8)	95

Oliver Tomkins CE VA Junior School, Toothill

Ingso Bega (9)	96
Zuzanna Rusek (9)	97
Deion Fiaka	98
Emanuella Sousa (9)	99
Aryah Ahmed (10)	100
Asher Desouza (10)	101
Lucas Campanha	102
Thomas Jones (9)	103
Viaan Deepak (9)	104
Olivier S (9)	105
Verity Lockwood (9)	106
Shalom Mutanhaurwa (10)	107
Theo Hepburn-Smith (10)	108
Kaycee Boateng (10)	109
Chloe-Maree Yon (10)	110
Lena Gozdz (9)	111
Jonathan Booton (9)	112
Oliwia Godlewska (10)	113
Lily-Mae Boulter (9)	114
Olivia Olubajo (9)	115
Erin O'Callaghan (10)	116
Ruby Godsell (9)	117
Maya Bass (9)	118
Ella-Louise Ward (9)	119
Ilarna Breslin (9)	120

The Free School Norwich, Norwich

Aavya Agarwal (8)	121
Jessica Thomas (8)	122
Nina Litwa (8)	124
Shreejay Manoj (8)	126
Oluwadara Kehinde (9)	128
Xenia Cotruta (9)	129
Phong Nguyen (8)	130
Advay Jain (8)	131

Ashish Madarapu (9)	132
Alfie Reid (8)	133
Skye Bramley (9)	134
Evelyn Smithson (9)	135
Bella Atkinson-Neill (9)	136
Sam Emmins (9)	137
Lyla Hawes (9)	138
Lee Codling (9)	139
Willow Davison (8)	140
Amelie Airgibi (9)	141
Yolandi-Joan Reynolds (8)	142
Samuel Allen (8)	143
Rufus Rix (8)	144
Isaac Butler (8)	145

The Woodlands Community Primary School, Glascote

Ellie Clamp (10)	146
Leila Morrissey (7)	148
Betsy Whiston (10)	149
Amelia Sleet (10)	150
Jacob Morrissey (10)	152
Sienna Nika (9)	154
Iyla Ford (10)	155
Margot Clark Macnab (7)	156
Evelae Amiss (8)	158
Bethany Milligan (7)	159
Lily-Ann Woolley (7)	160
Alexi-Grace Jones (10)	161
Laura Merrall (7)	162
Sid Chester (10)	163
Ella Jarratt (8)	164
Lucy-Mae Goodfellow (10)	165
Isaac Sulka (8)	166
Isabel Poll (9)	167
Poppie Jackson (9)	168
Harriet Nicholls (8)	169
Oscar Wakelin (10)	170

Whalley CE Primary School, Whalley

Isabella Castle (9)	171
Benjamin Allen (10)	172
Harriet Parkin (9)	174
Sapphire Webster (10)	175
Danielle Bassett (10)	176

THE POEMS

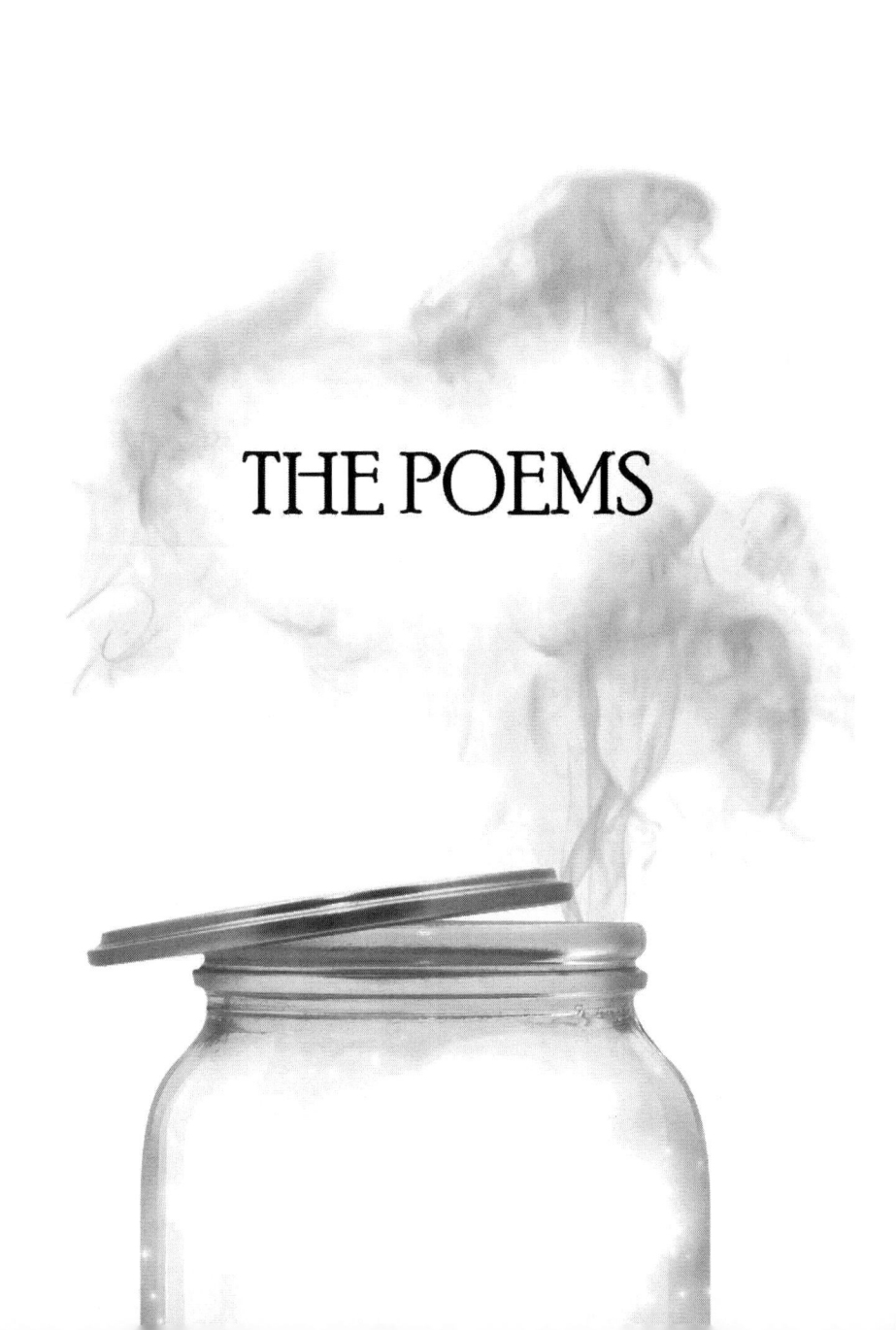

The Lost Boy

The boy was exploring the vast woodland
He looked left and right and stumbled across the misty wetland
He leapt fearlessly over the slippery stepping stones
As he came to his final step, he found a rotting pile of fish bones
He pondered why it died
He wondered if it cried
The boy gazed upon a pond filled with enormous lilies
For now, he was feeling rather chilly
So without hesitation, the boy left to get his coat
And found himself, staring at an abandoned broken boat
He rode curiously across the mystical pond
He majestically cast a spell just like a wizard
With a flick of a switch, the weather altered into a polar blizzard
The boy finally plucked up the courage to sail across the frozen pond
When he didn't realise he had lost his wand
He travelled to a roof over one's head
Where he quietly snuggled back into bed

Tamzin Buller (10)
Bridgwater College Academy, Bridgwater

My Dragon Dream

Every night, after I have Mum's kiss
My dream starts like this
Dragons flying everywhere,
Feeling the wind in my hair,
Pixies in the summer air
Start to make me stare.
Pong! Wait, that's the start
To my favourite song.
I lurked around,
Oh, what was that sound?
It was not a whistle, nor a cry
But maybe a song from someone shy.
It was a dragon glowing bright
In the moonlight
Looking fierce with might.
Her scales so shiny
But she herself was so tiny.
The moment I looked in her eyes, I knew
That she had the same pain I do.
She was trapped and wanted to be free,
Oh just like me.
I decided to call her Isla,
I didn't really know why either.

But she was beautiful like the name
And I knew she felt the same.
I hopped onto her back
And gave her a little smack,
We flew up high, we flew up low
Until we decided to go slow.
The sun was rising, it was bright
So we flew into the morning light.
Suddenly, I woke up to the lick of my pup.
It was nothing at all
Oh, I felt like a fool.
Magic isn't real, neither their song,
But I knew I was wrong.
Magic can be found everywhere,
But it is just not anywhere.

Erin McCallum (8)
Bridgwater College Academy, Bridgwater

Journey Beyond The Stars

I watched blue fluffy clouds drift across the sky,
Guided by the sun's gentle glow,
As I glided through the cushiony skies.

My crew laughed and sang.
We soared through space, claiming our territory.
But disbelief struck as we spied a floating boat.
How did it ever get here?

As we flew, my face turned delighted and gleeful.
As we navigated through obstacles ahead,
My crew equipped their space gear and glided off.
As I glided away, far away, to a distant planet far beyond.

The planets shone in glory while each of us separated
To find the golden treasure.
We had only one chance and we couldn't mess up!
We came this far and couldn't lead to failure.

But, finally, we found it!
We all then glided back up, feeling proud of ourselves.
I wondered if this adventure would ever come to an end.

Emilis Kisel (11)
Bridgwater College Academy, Bridgwater

My Medal!

Snuggled up in my bed, I started to dream,
I dreamed about fairies, I dreamed about frogs,
I dreamed about wizards, I dreamed about dogs.
Then the most wildest, wondrous dream came to me
Something I could only dream of going
But could it happen for real?
Could I win a medal or would I have to settle?
There I was at the Olympic Games
There were thousands of people, shouting all sorts of names.
I stood at the start line, ready to race
I jumped in the pool, taking my place.
I swam and swam with all my might,
I wasn't going down without a fight.
As I reached the edge of the pool, it was my time to shine,
I'd come in first place, the medal was mine.
I woke up suddenly and jumped out of bed,
Realising it was all in my head
But someday, I will be a champion swimmer,
Because I was born to be a winner.

Olivia Aldridge (9)
Bridgwater College Academy, Bridgwater

Escape

Nibble, nibble, hop!
Twitching whiskers that will never stop!
Ears on the floor that go flop
Fuzzy ears on the floor
Need to stop them before they go out of the door
Too late they've gone away
So I had to wait for another day
I cried so much that I was in pain
So I got up and went down the lane
When Mum woke up, I was back
But victory was what I lack
When I was gone, Mum made toast but now it's black
That evening I got a knock on my door
Then that was when I saw
My rabbits were back
And in the correct habitat
Then I said, "Thank you, I'll never lose them again."
And then I picked up a pen
And wrote them a letter.

Jessica Wilkin (7)
Bridgwater College Academy, Bridgwater

Take A Trip To Hogwarts

I can see the wizardly and magical Hogwarts.
I can see Harry Potter and his wondrous friends.
I can see the gorgeous views of Hogwarts.

Me and my friend will go and explore;
Won't you come with me?
On our majestic adventure, I have butterflies in my tummy
And bubbles of super-duper happiness burst inside of me.

As I walk in, I see the crazy moving pictures
And the changing position of staircases.
I walked through the Great Hall doors as they burst open.

We all walk in with pride as we all show off our new uniforms.
With joy and happiness, I see the Harry Potter actors!
I think I am going to faint!
Am I dreaming? Is this real?

Amelia Bowers (10)
Bridgwater College Academy, Bridgwater

Lost In Time

Walking through the woods as the sun begins to fade
Let's go back in time to another decade
Let's go to 1600 AD and discover history
Or discover another mystery.

Let's visit the Romans, or maybe not
Or go to 1914, when the First World War was fought
How about we visit 805 CE, when the first hospital was built
Or 3250 BCE, when the vase was invented.

Let's go back to 2019, okay never mind
How about 1879, when the first bulb was wired
That's enough history for one day
Let's play again sometime, what do you say?

Abigail Palasti (10)
Bridgwater College Academy, Bridgwater

The Prince And Princess

The prince and the princess were all alone in the dark forest.
They turned on the flashlight to see a big scary dragon,
With fire coming out of its mouth.

They ran all the way back to the castle
Where they hid away,
Because the dragon was trying to burn down the castle.

The dragon said, "If you don't let me in,
I'll huff and I'll puff until I blow your castle down!"

The dragon blew the castle down
And the prince and princess were nowhere to be found.

Lily-May Stockham (9)
Bridgwater College Academy, Bridgwater

Trigger, Mine And Sophie's Real Horse

In my dream, I had a horse.
His name is Trigger.
He stomps his hooves and it looks like he has been a digger.
Trigger is my real-life horse.
When he runs, it is with force.
Trigger lives at Alastone Court.
Trigger is my horse.
Me and Sophie my best friend
Go to Alastone Court and she has the same horse.
Called Trigger.
Trigger can dance and prance.
He's handsome too and likes to be with you.
I hope I win, I tried my best
But if not, at least
It was
Fun.

Nara Leigh Black (8)
Bridgwater College Academy, Bridgwater

Fairy Dancers

In my dreams every night
Fairy dancers dance through the light
They fly with colours bright
Dressing up and playing
One by one, they pass me doing ballet
Marissa was holding a bouquet
Probably for a wedding day
Fairy weddings are the best
All the shops get a rest
I think I would be a guest
They give you a power
Like all the rest.

Indie Tottle (9)
Bridgwater College Academy, Bridgwater

Away In The Meadows

Where am I?
Where could I be?
What can I smell?
What can I see?

I am in a meadow
Bright as can be
Is that a lion?
Or a little bee?

Am I sad or
Am I happy?
I don't know
But the lion's name is Sappy

It made me happy
Not sad
But the truth is
Today was rad.

Izabella Clarke (11)
Bridgwater College Academy, Bridgwater

True Love

A princess was in love
But when she looked above
A pirate was holding a dove
And the pirate that was holding the dove, Zack was in love
Both of them found each other's gloves
Both of them meet to give each other the gloves
And both of them find true love.

Alice Walford (8)
Bridgwater College Academy, Bridgwater

Dreams

D rifting off to sleep tonight
R eading in the moonlight
E very time I close my eyes
A nother dream I memorise
M e and my dreams together
S o memories last forever.

Lacey-Rose Peploe (10)
Bridgwater College Academy, Bridgwater

Artist

A rray of colours
R ustic vibes
T he sunset
I n the horizon
S lowly covering my canvas
T hen on my wall it goes, catching people's eye.

Scarlett Finn (10)
Bridgwater College Academy, Bridgwater

WWII Dreams

I awaken from my slumber
To hear heavy thunder
My eyes start to wake
I feel a giant quake
My head starts to pound
I hear strange sounds
I look to the left
I look to the right
Afraid that I will see a horrible sight
Is it real or in my mind?
Why can't I dream about people who are kind?
The poppies that were so bright
Have dimmed within the moonlight
There is a distant rumble in the ground
I feel like I'm lost and I will never be found
Is this how they felt?
When I wake up, I ponder
The fate of so many, their loved ones left to wonder.

Emma Richards (10)
Brightwell cum Sotwell CE Primary School, Brightwell cum Sotwell

I Had A Dream

I had a dream,
That I was sleeping on clouds,
I closed my eyes,
I could hear birds singing and playing around,
I could also feel the clouds so soft,
I opened my eyes,
And stood up,
I could fly!
Both my legs were floating up,
I couldn't imagine that I could fly,
I've also wanted to fly for a long time already,
I couldn't imagine it was really happening to me.
Suddenly, I slowly floated down to the town,
And I saw a bunch of lights glowing,
I closed my eyes,
When I woke up, I was still lying on my bed.

Ariel To (10)
Brightwell cum Sotwell CE Primary School, Brightwell cum Sotwell

My Red Kite

In my dreams every night
I dream I have a big red kite
I bring it out to play in the park
Whoosh! Off it goes just like a lark
Crash! It fell into a nearby tree
I fly over to the tree as fast as can be
Did I not say I could fly? How silly of me!
I climb to the top as eager as can be
Suddenly I see a glimpse of red in the next tree
I fly over to the next tree and pull out my kite
Luckily it's alright
I climb down from the tree
As happy as can be
I hold onto the handle
And let my kite free.

Ziva Osman (10)
Brightwell cum Sotwell CE Primary School, Brightwell cum Sotwell

Dreams

Sleep, the best time of the day.
You let all the problems float away.
When I'm nestled up in my bed,
I wonder what stories will take place in my head.

There could be anything in my dreams tonight.
I could meet a dinosaur and take flight.
I could become queen or turn into a bean.
I could go to Hogwarts and battle Voldemort.

When it's bedtime, finally,
I see a dream, just for me!
Until bedtime, I'll have to wait.
Now my dream is up to fate.

Maeve Norfolk (10)
Brightwell cum Sotwell CE Primary School, Brightwell cum Sotwell

Two Friends Lost In The Woods

Playing in the woods
With my best friend
Having an amazing time
We don't want it to end

The sun is going down
It's getting really dark
Hearing spooky noises
A dog has started to bark

We run really fast
Rustling leaves under our feet
Without looking back
We are now fast asleep

But those dark woods
Won't make us scream
We are tucked in bed
It was all just a dream.

Abbie Prior (10)
Brightwell cum Sotwell CE Primary School, Brightwell cum Sotwell

Alone

As I close my eyes in my comfy bed,
A dream comes upon my head.
I'm strolling along the dark dusty street,
There's no noise, not even a peep.
It's all dark, no colours in sight,
Just shadows, no bright.
Everything's empty, no buildings around,
All I can feel is the wind on my hand.
Just when I feel so alone,
I wake up to find myself safe at home.

Allegra Benarr (10)
Brightwell cum Sotwell CE Primary School, Brightwell cum Sotwell

Everything

Running, racing, speed of light
Spinning, twirling, lost in mind
Teacher, pirate, footballer
Royalty, flying, superpower
Builders, dragons, astronauts
Unicorns, dinosaurs, I'm lost in thought
Spiders, monsters
Wizards, fairies, famous singers
It all varies, what do I want to be?
It's always changing
But I know I will always be... amazing

Molly Horrocks (10)
Brightwell cum Sotwell CE Primary School, Brightwell cum Sotwell

Nightmare

I stir and stir,
I'm in fear.
I scream for help,
But no one hears.
Wait, something's moving in the mist,
Could it be my nightmare coming from the abyss?
It comes closer and closer,
I scream as loud as I can.
Until everything goes black,
I rub my eyes.
I'm back in my room,
But my mind has been telling lies.

Maggie Horrocks (10)
Brightwell cum Sotwell CE Primary School, Brightwell cum Sotwell

All Alone

When I wake up, I am all alone,
No other human beings, not even a clone.
The houses are abandoned, the work is at rest,
There are animals to hunt, time to put my skills to the test.
Oh what is that, another human over there?
I need to get there quick.
"Ow! What the?" I say,
As they give me a kick!

Molly Smith de Brito (10)
Brightwell cum Sotwell CE Primary School, Brightwell cum Sotwell

Dancer

D riving beat fills the room,
A rms moving with flair,
N ow my body feels the tune, I
C hase through the air,
E yes closed, I'm on the stage,
R eally happy that I'm there.

Molly Brack (9)
Brightwell cum Sotwell CE Primary School, Brightwell cum Sotwell

The Mysterious Dream

One lonely night,
There was this terrible sight,
It was very bright,
Because it was an unknown fright!

Somehow, I landed on this grand land,
It had dirty, crusty sand,
Can you guess what I found?

There was some puffy smoke,
I hoped it was a hilarious joke,
So I went to go have a nosy poke.

I had this dread,
I really wished I was curled up in my bed,
I had an urge to be fed,
Even if it was dried bread!

Suddenly, there was this face,
It looked as if it wanted to chase,
Was it on a secret case?

Aminah Majid (9)
Greenleaf Primary School, London

Rainbow Unicorns

R unning through fields of unicorns
A nd rainbow horns
I love to jump and play
N ow now, not today
B ecause it's a rainy day
O h no, I'm sad
W hat should I do now?

U nhappy, I think of what to do
N ow I ask Mum,
I ask everyone but they don't know
C an I think of something?
O h now I know
R ight now I'm sleepy, I'll play tomorrow
N ighty, night
S leep tight.

Anam Husain (10)
Greenleaf Primary School, London

Ice And Fire

I ce cubes falling from Antarctica
C old takes over the country
E arly mornings turn into snow storms.

A nd the coldest of weather takes over
N ight-times are like your worst nightmares all in one
D awn, now you're burning like fire.

F ire comes, and all your goosebumps disappear
I t's burning hot
R ight now, you wish for the cold of before
E agles fly sky-high, giving shivers down my spine.

Inaya Dhami (9)
Greenleaf Primary School, London

Imposters

In the infinite void of space, many are scared
Many want to hide, but fear is shared
Plenty of astronauts onboard dying one by one
One more second, then another kill is done
Someone is the murderer, but nobody knows who
Try and fail, because they're after you
Only one more spaceman is alive,
You run and try so hard to hide,
But the last thing you see is sharp knives,
Then you fall asleep.

Sophia Ellin (10)
Greenleaf Primary School, London

The Hero And The Hunter

I look up to the sky to find hues of purple and blue clouds.
Making my way, I stare at the scenery.
I see other creatures staring back at me.
I take a rest in the clearing.
I see the animals retreating.
Look up and see a dragon hunter
With a manic grin across his face.
He plans to steal the dragons
And make this world a waste.
With all my might, I try and shoo him away.
Sadly, it doesn't work.
I get a friend to help with this quest,
Hoping he will say yes.
I make a wish hoping it'll come true.
"I wish for this world to be safe and me too,"
I whisper to myself.
I stride off ready for battle,
My griffin alongside of me.
We hide behind a bush
Until he's distracted.
We make our move
Hoping nothing bad has reacted.

After a long, gruesome battle
We win and save the dragons.
Very pleased with myself
I make my way home
Until Silverwing stops me.
She gives me a gift to say thank you.
It turns out I'm a hero.
I say my farewells and leave through the door.
I open my eyes to see it was a dream.
But I know I'm still a hero in reality.

Veerangana Saraiya (10)
Larchfield Primary & Nursery School, Maidenhead

The Enchanted Forest

The day rushed by so fast,
It seemed my treats would not last!
I scrambled to my feet,
And then I heard a deafening drum beat!
It was so loud I could barely hear,
When something amazing did appear!
A dozen fairies in front of my eyes
Leaving a trail of... dead butterflies!
I tried to run but was stuck in my grasp,
The only thing I could do was gasp!
Fairies from all over heard the sound
And then they captured me with a hound!
They put me in a dungeon, oh so dull
Where there were some bones and a skull!
Then I opened my eyes,
And, to my surprise,
It was all just another dream.

Hannah Carvalho (9)
Larchfield Primary & Nursery School, Maidenhead

The Thing

Something was there
Coming for them
Running and running
As fast as they could
Not turning back
Not a second later
The thing could have come and ate her.

Kenza Olarewaju (9)
Larchfield Primary & Nursery School, Maidenhead

Untitled

Once upon an endless night,
The world turns ever so bright,
With children singing and dancing in delight,
Wonderful things come into sight.

Blades of grass dance in the breeze,
Mystical creatures pop up from behind luscious evergreen trees,
With powers unknown to humankind,
And they asked me to help them survive.

I spot something on their bodies,
It looks like they've been hit by lorries,
Weak and still on the ground they are,
How did this happen? This is so bizarre.

I will help you, I declare,
I shall make haste and take great care,
I run off in search of the magical cure,
I will make sure their health is secure.

I come back with magical fruit,
They take a bite and spring back to life,
Suddenly, I wake back up in bed,
To realise that it was all just a dream.

Louis Garner (11)
Manea Community Primary School, Manea

Once Upon A Dream

I was in a football stadium with lots of twisty twirls.
After the football match, I began to run
But I could not be found.
But then I travelled and travelled to a cave
And into the cave
And inside I found a dragon.
We went out to lunch twenty years later.
I was still there forty years later.
I was free, I could finally see
I wasn't going back to that lunch place
Because he might have seen that I was scared.
Some more twists and twirls.
To another cave.
But it was a different dragon
It was black and white.
The dragon and I went to Tesco
'Cause we got hash browns.
Then when we ate that
We went to the movies to watch Super Pets
It was really good.
But we got kicked out of the movie
Because he kept sneezing fire on the people in front.

Ronnie Richardson (8)
Manea Community Primary School, Manea

Pet Hotel

Far away, in a magical land
A pet hotel fosters pets
Before people buy them!
This hotel lets them roam about!
When you're there,
You won't have to pay.
You will have to go in,
Ask for an animal and it will appear!
Amazing things happen here,
Anything is possible!
Even if you make an animal up
And I don't know,
You will get it!
Whatever you wish, you will keep
If you want to work here,
You will sleep in the rooms above!
(That aren't made out of food)
The walls change colour in the dorms!
Around here, there are no storms!
You should come here
I'm waiting for you!

Don't forget every animal is here
Oh, and service is very quick.
(Make an animal up).

Violet Ronald (8)
Manea Community Primary School, Manea

Live Night Woods

L ying is bad, but it's better than someone going missing.
I n the woods, I was just walking until a stop
V egetable on the ground, I kept walking.
E vil, evil! Who did that? It's a waste.

N o one was in the woods, well that's what I thought.
I n the trees, there was a blanket, it looked familiar.
G oing closer, the person looked familiar.
H ere, what happened? Two days ago, my sister went missing.
T he things with the person looked familiar.

W ow, was it my sister? I went closer.
O h, it is my sister, Lucy.
O h, I did miss her.
D id she recognise me?
S is, are you okay?

Abbey Proctor (9)
Manea Community Primary School, Manea

Symbols Of Me

A purple haze, a mist, a dream,
Things look grey but they're not what they seem,
A shadow bounds from the fog,
Silver fur stood on a log,
A pink, little nose, darling paws,
It hops forwards on all fours.

A rabbit! Warm as forgiving love,
Watching over my friends from above,
I know he'll always be there,
For each other, we'll always care.

We walk together, paw in hand,
As joy spreads throughout the land,
Colour rockets, fast as my mind,
Showing everything as happy and kind.

Then we come across a house,
Tall and wide, a smile, not a grouse,
Shaking its shaggy shoulders covered in moss,
I feel protected, never with loss.

Lorna Garlick (11)
Manea Community Primary School, Manea

Stars! And Night Sky!

S tunning stars up above,
T ill dark, all I see is a dove,
A bove my head are shooting stars going past,
R ivers swaying, that's it at last,
S parkling moon comes out at noon.

N ight sky is so far but so high,
I n a blink of an eye it's so dark,
G oodnight, the moon is so
H igh above, the stars are so bright,
T onight I'll look out my window to look for shooting stars.

S prinkling rain makes the clouds dewy,
K ind hearts turn in for the night, whilst the brave stay awake and watch the moonlight,
Y awning while the stars start to appear, dreaming of the sky being so clear.

Evie Marshall (10)
Manea Community Primary School, Manea

Once Upon A Silent Night

Once upon a silent night,
I just manage to snuggle up tight
My eyes close
Suddenly, my sweet dreams arose
Cotton candy clouds drift through the sky
Blossom trees sway up super high
The clock turns to midnight
The sweet dreams are gone
Now it's time for the hard one
This night will be like no other
No one's hand to hold, no mother
Let's just say I'll be alright
And hope to survive the night
Killer clowns chase me
I climb up a big tree
Realising this is the end
They shake the branch and send me flying
This was me dying
I hit the floor
And wake up in my bed
With a cold cloth lying on my hot head.

Maisie Law (10)
Manea Community Primary School, Manea

Forest Friends

F orests are great places to have adventures.
O ne of the world's biggest forests is the Amazon.
R emember to take care of our forests.
E lements such as water, wind and earth are in the forest.
S o many different plants live in the forest.
T rees need to stop being cut down.

F eel free to take a trip to your forest.
R eally should we be littering?
I n any way possible let's help out our forests.
E very forest should be treated with respect.
N o forest should have litter.
D own in the forest, my beautiful creatures.
S quirrels are mostly spotted in forests.

Charlie Harding (10)
Manea Community Primary School, Manea

I Met A Mermaid

In my bed tonight,
I closed my eyes and saw a colourful light.
I opened them, I was at a beach!
I had a picnic with sandwiches, mango and a peach.
After that, I had a swim,
The water was full to the brim!
I swam to the soft white sand,
Through the green seaweed and past the fish.
I went back up for air,
And... oh no! I was lost!
I couldn't see the lovely beach with the golden sand!
I went back down again... I saw a mermaid with a waving hand!
Then, she started swimming,
I thought for a moment, and I began following.
I went back up... and I saw the beach,
The lovely beach, with the golden sand!

Clara Bembridge (9)
Manea Community Primary School, Manea

Angry Cats

In my dreams, I have every night,
Is a galaxy with stars so bright,
If you take your eyes off the sky,
The one with stars ever so high,
You will see a cat,
Loads of those cuties,
But not cats,
Angry cats,
In your house made of confetti cake,
Is an angry cat,
Wearing a hat,
Sleeping on a catnip mat,
And has a kitten friend playing with a rat,
Time for dinner,
Tuna for tea,
None for me,
Munch, munch, munch,
They ate a bunch,
No angry cats,
Now happy cats,
playing with a happy rat,
Happy catnip mats and happy hats.

Molly Grannell (10)
Manea Community Primary School, Manea

Dream Horse

Late at night,
I ride my dream horse
She's set a course
We ride through seas
And over cities.
My friends look in shock
I wave back in my flowery frock
Then she takes me to her home
Long time we've flown
Her family couldn't have been kinder
Day's approaching
She is fading
"I must take you home!"
"Okay," I sigh
We ride off home
Past witches and fairies
By the time I'm home
She's nearly dust
"Goodbye, my friend!"
"See you tomorrow, Moonbeam!"

Raine Wilkes (10)
Manea Community Primary School, Manea

Dreams Come Every Night

Once upon a dream,
Cotton candy clouds fly through the sky,
Blossom trees sway up high,
Bees buzz and butterflies land,
And I'm happy that I'm once found,
Once upon a nightmare,
Wind whistles in my ears,
I am now faced with my fears,
I hear screams,
So I definitely don't want ice cream,
Green goblins screech,
My hand tries to reach,
But a flower dies,
And I burst into cries,
For the petals that lie,
Are no longer alive,
I wake up,
Staring at my cup,
Realising it was just a nightmare.

Melody Millward (11)
Manea Community Primary School, Manea

Once Upon A Dream

Once upon a dream,
I found myself in a world, where up above me the sky swirled and swirled.
The grass that grew beneath me, stretched as far as I could see.
I was surrounded by creatures that I couldn't possibly name.
Each one was different, not one was the same.
Then as I wandered, I came across a cave.
Darkness was my only fear.
I had to be brave.
Then from the cave came two amber eyes.
Me, a small child, could not compare to its size.
In pure terror I turned and fled.
Only to find myself safe in bed.

Sienna Scarff (10)
Manea Community Primary School, Manea

My Fishing World

In this dream, the water was dancing,
As I reeled in the fish, colourful like a rainbow,
The trees howling, like a husky,
The gravel was singing,
The birds flew past like supercars,
The cars popped like balloons,
The seaweed wrapped around each other like ropes,
The fish jumped into the air like jets,
The kingfish sat on the bottom,
Like the king on his throne,
I looked up to see the blue sky, like the sea,
What I saw was all a dream,
The alarms screamed,
I woke up, it was all a dream.

Noah Evans (9)
Manea Community Primary School, Manea

The Clown

In a deep dark forest where once I land,
I think this place should be banned.
Daring trees spread as far as I can see,
This is, this is the place I dare to be.
I turned in despair as I hear a twig snap,
I see a smile from ear to ear with one big gap!

Running with speed it comes for me,
I close my eyes and count one, two, three.
I am lying down, I wonder why.
Lying stiff, I open one eye.

I have a feeling soon I might be dead,
Until I realise I am tucked up in my bed.

Emily Swinden (10)
Manea Community Primary School, Manea

Dreamland

When I fall asleep at night,
I run from my comfy bed,
To seek sparkling moonlight,
All worries become dead.

When I fall asleep at night,
Bright colours dance around,
This strange, distant land,
Has finally been found.

When I fall asleep at night,
Cotton candy clouds hover in the starlit sky,
This world a place of wonder.

When I fall asleep at night,
Anything can happen,
You can fly up high,
Do anything you imagine,
Once upon a dream.

Lydia Lane (11)
Manea Community Primary School, Manea

Nightmares

N ight has arrived, you scream to death.
I 'm lost, no one is here to keep me company.
G lancing left and right, all I can see is darkness!
H ow did I get here in this scariness?
T errifyingly, I take a step forward into the darkness.
M idnight has struck, I'm scared.
A rgh! Someone's chasing me!
R unning as fast as I can
E ventually, they stop chasing me.
S uddenly, I wake up to find out I am safe at home in bed.

Izi Barnes-Stubbins (9)
Manea Community Primary School, Manea

Do Robots Dream Of Eternal Sleep?

Do robots dream of eternal sleep?
Do robots even think?
Do they even want to take over?
Do we overthink their power?

Do robots dream of eternal sleep?
Do robots feel emotions?
Do they feel love at all?
Do they want to steal our lives?

Answer, answer, please answer me,
Do robots ever want to be free?
Do robots dream of eternal sleep?
Once upon a dream.

The world is your canvas,
So pick up your brush and paint happiness.

Theodore Kerans (11)
Manea Community Primary School, Manea

Me And Sundee

I woke and found myself in the fungle.
I was all alone so I went to explore.
On the way, I accidentally stepped on a green mushroom.
It made a poison so I held my breath, closed my eyes and ran away.
I wasn't looking where I was going
So I accidentally bumped into Sundee and his idiotic friends.
I was so happy, I asked Sundee and his friends and they all said, "Yes."
Everyone except Biffle.
Biffle was scared because he thought I was the imposter.

Harley Young (8)
Manea Community Primary School, Manea

Dream

Once upon a dream, I find myself in a far-off world
Around me, colours swim and swirl
As I stare a creature lands
With giant wings and crystal eyes
And golden horns of incredible size
Its scales are aquamarine
With flecks of emerald-green.

As I wait with fear and glee
I reach out and touch its snout
Then something incredible happens
Its helmet starts to glow a brilliant gold
Then I know what to do
So I name it Dream.

Lily O'Reilly (10)
Manea Community Primary School, Manea

Constellations

Once upon a dream,
As the stars up high will gleam,
I knew all I had to be,
Was me.
Glistening above the great blue sea,
Was a big, golden, fat monkey,
Looking up at me,
Saying, "Hello, I can see you!"
Then there were two,
Two geese floated around the pond with their
Legs in the air,
Getting the whole world to stare.
I then found out I was in my bed,
Lots of emotions were going through my head.

Josie McKew (9)
Manea Community Primary School, Manea

Once Upon A Dream

On a silent night,
Amazing things take flight,
Dinosaurs and dragons in the sunny light,
On a silent night.

When the wind blows,
In my dreams at night,
Crunchy leaves fly around me,
When the wind blows.

As I lie in my bed at night,
I know I liked my dream,
The daylight will come soon,
The sun instead of the moon,
The morning has begun,
Lots in the long day to come.

Once upon a dream.

Alice Bembridge (11)
Manea Community Primary School, Manea

The Slime Pit

Once upon a dream,
I got pulled into a slime pit,
My lungs were filled with slime,
And I could not move in time
To dodge all the grime,
Followed by slime.
I glimpse red eyes, now I'm terrified.
Now I'm grabbed tight, what's going on?
I see a bright light, what's going on?
Oh, it's just my night light.
I pleasantly realise it was all just a dream.
But then I hear a scream, was it just a dream?

Jack Turner (11)
Manea Community Primary School, Manea

Emirates

As Saka dribbles and shoots,
The opposing fans shout, "Boo!"
Ramsdale gets hit in the face,
But then makes a brilliant save!
As Rice drives by,
He will be floating in the sky,
Ødegaard does a volley,
Then a roly-poly,
As the fans shout, "Move back!"
The opposing fans give a bit of lack,
The opposing player grabs Nelson's back,
He turns around and gives them a smack!

Mia Stock (10)
Manea Community Primary School, Manea

What Will Happen Next Year?

In my dreams every night,
I see you there, I'm at home,
I open my eyes, you disappear,
Everything is warm,
I'll be back maybe tonight,
Maybe next year.

In my dreams every night,
The world isn't what it seems,
We're maybe in a video game,
Where we go into the night,
There is a lot of light,
With the stars
Shining bright.

Tonight I will lie,
In my bed to wonder.

Mia Scarff (10)
Manea Community Primary School, Manea

Your Inner Self

Dancing spirits are on the ground.
They are not mostly found.
Dragons roaring loud.
Lions standing proud.
Astronauts are flying to the moon.
I'm sure I'll see them soon.
I feel really calm.
And coconuts are in my palm.
I'll see them at noon.
I'm going to the beach.
I'll eat a peach.
Always believe in yourself.
And feel your inner self.

Oliver McGee (8)
Manea Community Primary School, Manea

Fire

F ire is giving me a warm smile
I n the night while I am
R eading an awesome book that takes me to another world, looking at
E very page it warms me up and I grow.

B lowing off the dust of a book
L oving every page, looking
A t the pictures on the pages
Z ooming through the book, I've read
E very single page!

Roman Boyce (9)
Manea Community Primary School, Manea

An Amazing World

M ore than just a land
A beautiful, fascinating plan
L oads of things to see and do
A mazing oceans and tropical dew
Y ou are hot, you are tired, let's sit down for food
S picy flavours that match my adventures
I magining an amazing world, but stir
A nd find myself tucked away in bed to see another dream come true.

Aryanna Scarff (8)
Manea Community Primary School, Manea

The Food War

The apples and pears have declared war
On the fish fingers and pies.
Everywhere has been destroyed
Fish Finger Palace is left and we have to defend it.
Air raid sirens fill the air.
Stuka dive bomber flies close
By then, some bombs fly by.
A gun stretches up high.
Tiger tanks blow up planes
The wrecks throwing men
And the fight is over and we won.

Dennis Dean (8)
Manea Community Primary School, Manea

My Magic Dragon

Once upon a dream, flying high in the sky
Me and my dragon in the sky
She lives in the dreamy night clouds
Flying low and high
Flying in space
Her blue scales and lilac eyes
She's dreaming
And so am I
We fly across the blue sea
Suddenly we see a monkey
She flies back home and goes to sleep
I wake up in my bed
Soon to fall asleep.

Georgia Polley (10)
Manea Community Primary School, Manea

A Dream Land

A big portal appears, it's green-black.

D ark means I am asleep
R ed land of happiness
E arth is gone, not in sight
A s I open my eyes
M y eyes are so red.

L anding on Mars
A gust of dust comes
N ow my book comes alive
D olls are alive (the book said).

Charlie Fyson (11)
Manea Community Primary School, Manea

In The Night I Had A Fright

In the night,
I had quite a fright,
I was in a tree,
There was just so much to see,
Dragons flying in the sky,
Across the sky, they're just so high,
Wizards doing spells,
Wizards hiding in wells,
Fairies playing with bells,
Fairies relaxing in cells,
Then I woke up,
And it was just a dream,
Once upon a dream.

Elliot Skeggs (10)
Manea Community Primary School, Manea

Untitled

In my dreams every night
Arm wrestles at a big stadium trying to win every fight
Dreaming about adventures to complete every night
I was dreaming about a magical land and in this land there are lots of competitions
I was the dream hero and everyone was trying to win against me
It was a hard match but I did not want to give up.

Harris Farrer (7)
Manea Community Primary School, Manea

Untitled

To be a perfect boxer, you have to be really fit.
You have to be as sneaky as a fox.
You have to be as fast as a heartbeat.
Be able to take a punch.
Doesn't matter if he is a butch
The ring hugs you and keeps you safe.
You have to remember to be brave.
Boxing gloves protect your hands.
And fit like bands.

Alfie Youfens (11)
Manea Community Primary School, Manea

Magic Land

Up above the sky
There's a magical land
Where angels have
Extinct animals as pets.
Angels play on the fluffy clouds
While pterodactyls glide
Through the heavenly land.
All the angels always smile
Because they always have fun
With the animals.
Dinosaurs roam the land peacefully
And are harmless.

Darcy Bradford (8)
Manea Community Primary School, Manea

What Am I?

A kennings poem

Fire breather
Trick performer
Meat chomper
Tree bumper
Scale wearer
Eye changer
Poo exploder
Dragon footer
Dragon flyer
Claw scratcher
Tail whipper
Steam breather
Eye explorer
Spike cutter
Three headed
Bone cruncher
Meat eater
Flame thrower
Claw kicker.

Ronnie Hassall (7)
Manea Community Primary School, Manea

Dancing Dog

Shutting my eyes, going to sleep
Then I wake up in a
Mythical dream, not fright just light
Fluffy white dogs dancing
In the night-time sky.

Every night, my dreams are
Full of light, dancing dogs
Fill me with pride
My dreams have no fright
Just light, I see them
Without a
Fright.

Poppy Smith (11)
Manea Community Primary School, Manea

Hogwarts

H arry is a great wizard
O h, no! I am being turned into a cat!
G o on Hermione, you got this.
W arning you... Expelliarmus!
A giant spider is coming
R ack of cats which were once teachers
T eachers mewing like cats
S tars in the sky as I come to Hogwarts.

Rowan Clegg (7)
Manea Community Primary School, Manea

Dragon World

D ragons flew overhead.
R oars filled the air.
A dragon flew towards me, I said,
"**G** osh, you're big."
O ver his head tons and tons of baby dragons flew mentally!
N one of them attacked me.
S ome baby dragons came and played with me.

Charlie Newsmith (8)
Manea Community Primary School, Manea

Being A Famous Footballer

F antasic, muddy, rich, fast as a flash
O h no, they scored
O h how did they do that?
T hat they scored, I'm never giving up
B ut it's all about trying hard
A ll about how you play
L ovely and healthy, sporty
L ike a star.

Leon Garner (7)
Manea Community Primary School, Manea

Dragon Breath

Smoke in my eyes
Dragons in disguise
A cave as big as an ocean
Superheroes making magic potions
Spiders crawling up my back
Dragons flying around me
I give one a big smack
The dragon's face lights up in glee
I am safe and sound
In my bed, it is just a dream.

Isaac Beeken (10)
Manea Community Primary School, Manea

Football

Every time I close my eyes,
Shivers of excitement go down my spine
I always see the same thing
Fans cheering
The ball flying up the pitch
I kick it
Bang, top corner
3-2 win
What a game
Champions League win
Loads of fame

Once upon a dream.

Archie Ronald (10)
Manea Community Primary School, Manea

Untitled

D inosaurs are curious
I can touch my blue dinosaur
N ever step in front of a dinosaur
O scar's dinosaur
S o my dinosaurs are really scary
A ngry dinosaurs
U nderground fossils
R oaring dinosaurs.

Oscar Ash (7)
Manea Community Primary School, Manea

Dreams

D uring the night, I woke up in a fright,
R eading a terror from a mirror,
E nchanting night of the fright,
A sking upon the night for some light,
M easuring the meter of every letter,
S ometimes seeking lifetime dreaming.

Abby Calder (10)
Manea Community Primary School, Manea

Dino Killer

A kennings poem

Dino killer
Dino pooper
Dino computer
Dino eater
Dino stamper
Dino whacker
Dino runner
Dino sniffer
Dino licker
Dino drinker
Dino ruler
Dino appearance
Dino displayer
Dino doctor
Dino driller
Dino dino.

Jimmy Eric Dean Lane (9)
Manea Community Primary School, Manea

Nightmares

N ightmares,
I 'm scared,
G iant clowns are chasing me!
H aunted,
T he room was pitch-black,
M e,
A re chasing me,
R unning around,
E very time they scare me!
S cared.

Ivy Tasker (7)
Manea Community Primary School, Manea

Dream Hotel

When I go to bed every night,
I enter the dream hotel
All dreams are welcome, they say
I find my room, all dreams
A pony, sports, pets, clothes, food, Santa and more.

But when the dream ends
I go back to my bed
All ready for the day.

Emra Day (10)
Manea Community Primary School, Manea

Footballer

I need to have a trainer
To teach me how to be a footballer
We need strength
To be a footballer
Strong arms and legs
To throw and kick
And score goals and cool kicks
Like score goals out of the box
From the other goals
From far away.

Mason Lemmon (10)
Manea Community Primary School, Manea

Footballer

F ans crowding around
O n the football pitch
Ø degaard missed again
T he crowd went wild
B all
A round the pitch
L iverpool win the treble again
L ong way from home.

Jenson Day (9)
Manea Community Primary School, Manea

Dino Rider

A kennings poem

Dino chomper
Meat eater
Scale wearer
Tree rocker
Dino sharer
Great see-er
Great sniffer
Prey sharer
Food sniffer
Dino rider
Fish snatcher
Fast flyer
Supernova
Plant eater
Rock wrecker.

Farys Thompson (8)
Manea Community Primary School, Manea

Football

F un game to play
O utstanding sport
O ver the goal and into the crowd
T ackling to win the ball
B est sport ever
A thletic
L ots of goals
L earn skills at training.

Josh Skeggs (8)
Manea Community Primary School, Manea

Something Mythical

Fire, water, wind and nature.
Learning all their elements together.
Something mythical lies in
The magic forest, while me and
Britney Spears sing Toxic!
What am I?

Answer: An elemental dragon.

Imogen Lakin (8)
Manea Community Primary School, Manea

A Dancer

A humongous crowd gathered around me

D ancing around on the stage
A British dancer
N atural mover
C ircling and dancing
E xcellent dancer
R esilience.

Ella Harrison (8)
Manea Community Primary School, Manea

Flying Pirates

In my dreams,
Flying pirates I see,
Coming to me,
To seize my money.

They go so high,
Floating through the sky,
When they see a guy,
They raise their rapiers high!

Jake Lee (10)
Manea Community Primary School, Manea

My Pet German Sausage

My pet sausage, his name is German,
He lives in Birmingham,
He prays to Zeus,
He's friends with a goose,
He loves running,
But not jumping.
I sure do miss him.

Tyler Shadbolt (10)
Manea Community Primary School, Manea

The Spider Baller

Tiny black hairs sit upon his head,
Dreaming of him fills me with dread,
His eyes flicker from left to right,
Looking at him gives me a bite.

Big pincers!

Jesse Markowski (7)
Manea Community Primary School, Manea

The Magical Dragon

A dragon flew over the football stadium,
It blew flames over the crowd of people,
The people ran because of the dragon,
The footballers got off the pitch.

Kayden-Jack Barnes (7)
Manea Community Primary School, Manea

Beach

B eaches are fun,
E veryone loves the beach,
A t least me and Nigel do,
C ome to the beach,
H ave some fun.

Taylor Judd (11)
Manea Community Primary School, Manea

Rise Of The Pirates

A kennings poem

People killers
Monster fighters
Treasure hunters
Mean snarlers.

Charlie Doggett (8)
Manea Community Primary School, Manea

Once Upon A Dragon

A kennings poem

Colour changer
Fire breather
Bone crusher
Human crusher.

Jacob Drummond (8), Noah Kendall (7) & Tarley Brown (7)
Manea Community Primary School, Manea

Once Upon A Spider

A kennings poem

Web spinner
Fly catcher
Leg tickler
Hairy monster.

Ralph Daniel (8)
Manea Community Primary School, Manea

Space

Space is my place
Where every night I dream
About planets hanging in the sky.
I see planets are black, blue and white,
Oh, space is a wonderful delight.

Munching on Mars bars
I float in the sky,
I think about home as a special delight.
I'm lying in a sea of stars,
I see a huge bright light,
Shimmering in the air,

Lights flying through the sky,
It leads me there, into a big light,
Yawning, I go to sleep,
Dreaming about what it will be,
Waving goodbye,
I start to close my eyes to a nice delight.
A room right there, in my sleep,
I drift in space, thinking it feels weird.
Yawning, I wake up to find it was a dream,
Or was it?

Ingso Bega (9)
Oliver Tomkins CE VA Junior School, Toothill

The Secret!

S o I walked down to the basement and you won't guess what I saw. An
E nchanted door! It shone super bright, so I went in. It was a whole world of Disney
C ruella De Vil!
R afiki!
E lsa!
T he enchanted door led me here...

I walked around the place seeing more and more Disney characters.
Then I walked into a room with Rapunzel and it was my mom!
I thought she was with my friend, Loki, doing some wedding planning.
I didn't know what to think, especially about the questions.

Did my mom star in the Rapunzel movie or any other movies?
Is she a movie star?
And more importantly, is she a Disney princess?

Zuzanna Rusek (9)
Oliver Tomkins CE VA Junior School, Toothill

Keep Dreaming

K eep dreaming
E veryone you love and trust will support you
E veryone can see their dreams and themselves in the future
P erseverance is the key to dreams.

D ream and you'll believe
a **R** ound you, you see dreams and goals have been achieved
E ven when you're down, keep dreaming
A gain you dream you might change what you want to be, the
M ore you dream, the more you want to be
I know everyone's future is bright, everyone's
N ever back down, never give up
G ive your dreams a shot and keep dreaming.

Deion Fiaka
Oliver Tomkins CE VA Junior School, Toothill

Red Robin

R ound and round the lovely pine tree.
E choing whistles around the lovely pine tree.
D igging for a response of life at the lovely pine tree.

R eaching up his little wings at the lovely pine tree.
O n the blink of an eye, the red robin disappeared far away from the pine tree.
B ristol stopped there the red robin was next to a lovely pine tree.
I mmediately I tried to catch the red robin beside the lovely pine tree.
N o luck this time, see if you can catch him next time next to the lovely pine tree.

Emanuella Sousa (9)
Oliver Tomkins CE VA Junior School, Toothill

What Will I Dream?

What will I dream; what will I be?
Will I be asleep or in a willow tree?
Will I be confused or hurt,
Or maybe buried in dirt?
Will I be asleep in my bed,
Or will I just lie there in dread?
Will a monster sneak up on me,
Or will I just stand there and weep?
What will I see, what will I be?
Will I see my worst nightmares come true in front of me,
Or will I see eyes watching me?
Will I know, will I not?
Will I tie my hair in a knot?
Listen as I say my farewells,
While I drift off to sleep,
Just swear not to peek...

Aryah Ahmed (10)
Oliver Tomkins CE VA Junior School, Toothill

Cars

What brings you here?
It's time to cheer!
Cars are so cool,
That they make you drool.

The engines are so loud,
That you can't even shout,
They are louder than thunder,
With an F1 engine bandar.

It might be a lot of money,
But you'll ride it like a sweet bunny.
They look really good,
You will be shook by your money.

The wheels are so fast,
I feel like they're gonna blast,
They're faster than a blink of an eye,
But it's time to say goodbye.

Asher Desouza (10)
Oliver Tomkins CE VA Junior School, Toothill

The Big Dream

It was a big dream,
Four tall statues in the sky,
I was playing football with my friend,
Then a monster appeared
His name was Mr Bob,
He said that he would eat me,
I was really scared,
But then he said,
"If you don't want to be eaten then you need to do my challenges."
I said, "What are these challenges?"
He said that the first one was to bring him food,
I went to the food sky shop,
Then I bought the food.

Lucas Campanha
Oliver Tomkins CE VA Junior School, Toothill

Football

Football is a sport of roughness,
Although it takes some skill.
It just takes practice to get you over the top of that hill,
But as they say, practice makes perfect.
The practice might get rather hectic,
As people start to get mad.
After the game ends, you will be glad,
Even if you don't win the game.
It's not all about the game,
The game is just for fun.
If you just get it done,
I'm sure it will be great.

Thomas Jones (9)
Oliver Tomkins CE VA Junior School, Toothill

My Dream World

Once there was a magical world
It was filled with all kinds of tales
You could see colours which are swirled
Heavens are sighted from the trails
People could see witches flying and wizards using magical spells
With gods playing around the golden sand
Humankind feeling healthy and well
Creatures wandering around the forest
Habitants live with a smile on their face
All animals chorused
Fairies and elves lived with grace.

Viaan Deepak (9)
Oliver Tomkins CE VA Junior School, Toothill

Dragon Land

D ragons are amazing
R iding and riding in the sky
A n Iceland with blue and white dragons flying
G liding in the sky above
O ften flying dragons, but sometimes sea dragons
N ot sometimes bad, but good too

L anding swiftly
A giant ice mountain in the Iceland middle
N ice soaring through the skies
D ragon taming.

Olivier S (9)
Oliver Tomkins CE VA Junior School, Toothill

Polar Bears

P olaris, North Star diamond bright,
O verhead in the soot-black sky,
L and like a snow-covered blanket,
A rctic circles me in cold
R emote polar bear lands.

B lack skin hidden beneath dazzling white fur,
E ating boisterous blubbery seals,
A ir sniffing from miles away,
R aw, sharp paws,
S wimming for days, free!

Verity Lockwood (9)
Oliver Tomkins CE VA Junior School, Toothill

My Dream World

In my dreams, every night,
I see unicorns shining so bright,
Fairies smiling down at me,
As I twirl gracefully
Like a ballerina leaping in the air,
Feels like something should be there,
Then poof! many people appear;
A football player doing awesome skills,
Then I see the adult version of me
Being an empathetic surgeon,
Helping innocent people in need.

Shalom Mutanhaurwa (10)
Oliver Tomkins CE VA Junior School, Toothill

Space Rangers

There are nine planets that orbit the sun,
But people and animals live on just one.

I saw a spaceman in space,
Wearing a raincoat just in case.
I also saw a sandwich in space,
Backflipping all over the place.

Beautiful shooting stars,
I would like to put them in a jar.
Flying all around in space,
Put a helmet on to cover your face.

Theo Hepburn-Smith (10)
Oliver Tomkins CE VA Junior School, Toothill

My Dream

I look around to see
All that's around me
From unicorns, to dragons,
To soccer referees.
What shall I do,
In this world of imagination?
Roar! goes the dragon
That swirls around me,
Should I ride its back?
Seems good enough to me.
I open my eyes to see what's all around me,
I wonder what awaits...
We'll have to see!

Kaycee Boateng (10)
Oliver Tomkins CE VA Junior School, Toothill

Monsters! Monsters! Everywhere

M onsters! Monsters! Everywhere
O h look, one has crazy red hair
N aughty or nice, it's hard to tell
S tanding still like I'm under a spell
T alking a language, I cannot speak
E xhausted and yawning, I let out a shriek
R eal or not, I cannot tell
S hh, someone's coming, please don't yell.

Chloe-Maree Yon (10)
Oliver Tomkins CE VA Junior School, Toothill

Life Of Being A Singer

Stage glittery like the stars
People cheering happily
Hear the beat of clapping
My smile looking happier than ever.
I can see fans flashing their flashlights to get my attention
My members dancing with excitement
One fan by one, they pass me by
Signing autographs again and again
I wish one day that could actually happen without hesitation.

Lena Gozdz (9)
Oliver Tomkins CE VA Junior School, Toothill

Good Luck, Bad Luck

Down the roads, there is a school
Everywhere some kids get out of trouble
And others don't
What is the problem?
Are there favourite children
Or unliked children?
What a shame
That sounds like a you problem
Some people blame others
For doing something they haven't done
Poor children get accused
Would you like it?

Jonathan Booton (9)
Oliver Tomkins CE VA Junior School, Toothill

Fairies And Dragons

In my dreams, every night,
Fairies and dragons fly bright at night,
Faires and dragons all day long,
Make them be friends until the end.
Flying and passing magical potions,
One by one and to the next.
Fairies flying up the roof make dragons fly there too,
But really sadly, they disappear.
For now, they will perhaps come next year...

Oliwia Godlewska (10)
Oliver Tomkins CE VA Junior School, Toothill

The Swaying Beach

In the glistening sea, the palm trees swayed
And the clouds travelled along the clear air
The birds sang to any animal life
But no one, not even a bit of life
Heard the waves waving
And splashing into the Rocky Mountain
The deep, unknown ocean swished
And turned in many directions
But was still calm.

Lily-Mae Boulter (9)
Oliver Tomkins CE VA Junior School, Toothill

Dreams

Dreams are cool
I know it too
You can dream about life itself
Or even riding it too
I mean, it's your dream
Your rules
But sometimes it fools
And has to end now
Or you're down
Sometimes it gets cut short
But at least you had a dream
Believe it, sometimes dreams come true.

Olivia Olubajo (9)
Oliver Tomkins CE VA Junior School, Toothill

Memories

D reams always come to me when I need them
R eminding me of loved ones who are not with me now
E very pet to cross the rainbow bridge waiting to say hello again
A dog and a cat were the ones I loved and miss the most
M emories come to visit me in my dreams.

Erin O'Callaghan (10)
Oliver Tomkins CE VA Junior School, Toothill

I Meet A Fairy

Once upon a time, there was a girl with her dog
And she tripped over a log and found a frog
And she found a fairy and gave her a berry
And the fairy was nice and merry
And they became friends, and the berry
Made her a fairy, and the real fairy was
Wary of the dog.

Ruby Godsell (9)
Oliver Tomkins CE VA Junior School, Toothill

How To Be An F1 Driver

F1 driving, winning, willing for a winning,
F1 driver crashing and flashing, surfing,
Driving, flying in F1 driving,
Drive in the flight,
Price is nice all night,
You will like the price all night.

Maya Bass (9)
Oliver Tomkins CE VA Junior School, Toothill

Dragon And Unicorn

When I dream big at night
Dragons and unicorns in my sight
Zooming and flying round and round
Makes me think I'm lost
Glitter and sparkles fly and more.

Ella-Louise Ward (9)
Oliver Tomkins CE VA Junior School, Toothill

Foxes

Fox
Sneaky, sturdy
White, orange, red
Nocturnal, predator
Foxes.

Ilarna Breslin (9)
Oliver Tomkins CE VA Junior School, Toothill

A Unicorn Dream

I was in the big, damp tunnel;
I was lost.
I kept on walking until it stopped.
I opened the door, I couldn't believe my eyes,
There were unicorns in a forest that were saying, "Hi!"
I discovered different stuff, like fairies and moths!

But suddenly, I touched down to the unicorn
And she was squishy like a fluffy pillow.
The tree next to the unicorn was smooth as a tiny lamppost,
Like the one in my bedroom,
And the bees felt like string hanging up on the ceiling.

Suspiciously, my eyes started to open, it was weird as they were already open.
I started to yawn, but I was already awake,
There was no unicorn!
No forest!
No tunnel!
It was just a dream!

Aavya Agarwal (8)
The Free School Norwich, Norwich

Once Upon A Big Building

Once, I was on a building,
It was as tall as sixty double-decker buses,
On top of each other,
It was fun up there,
I wished I could fly,
Though I had a jacket with stars on,
Some boots, all shimmering pink,
Some trousers with blue hearts on,
And some gloves all shimmering with gold.

Once, I was on a building,
I was running across the building,
When I tripped and fell over the edge,
Argh! It was frightening,
I've fallen off something before,
But not from this high,
Argh!

Once, I was on a building,
But as I was about to hit the ground,
Argh! Someone caught me,
The building started to look like my bed,
My wardrobe, my shelf,
Then I realised my brother had his hands on my back,

The lights were turned on,
The kettle was boiled,
There was food on my lap,
My brother said his baby brother was here,
And it was all just a dream,
And his baby brother was in front of me.

Jessica Thomas (8)
The Free School Norwich, Norwich

I Can Do It!

"I can do it!" I repeat
Even though I'm petrified
The nightmarish cheer of the crowd is hair-raising
But when I realise who is going up next
It makes me shiver from head to toe
I repeat, "I can do it, I can do it!"

"I can do it!" I repeat
Even though I'm mounting now
Suspense is creeping in around
Zipping my mouth closed with glue
But then I realise my hands are sinking down!
But is that normal? I don't think so!

"I can do it!" I repeat
Even though I'm alighting now
Excitement breaking through
But the floor looks like mine!
It looks like mine, it can't be true
The world is shaking now!
But I pick up on some kind of siren.

It sounds oddly familiar
Oddly familiar, I say
Still, the siren carries on!
Until my eyes peel open!
It was all a dream.

Nina Litwa (8)
The Free School Norwich, Norwich

The Small Black Hole

I find a path leading to a small black hole,
I go closer,
I find a small, little mole.
The small, little mole goes into the small black hole,
I follow it into the small black hole,
It's dark, damp and dripping.
I am scared of the dark,
I am wet from the drips,
I crawl to the end of the small, black hole.

I see the end of the small black hole,
I see some light,
Is it the small black hole's light or the morning light?
The small, black hole's soil is softer,
I hear some noises,
Is that a tree stump, or is it my clock?
Is that a brick wall, or is it my wardrobe?
I don't know!

Am I lost?
I'm moving,
I'm itchy,
Is this the end?
Beep, beep, beep, beep,
Oh, it was just a dream.

Shreejay Manoj (8)
The Free School Norwich, Norwich

The Mysterious Treehouse

I woke up in a mysterious treehouse and looked around,
That was when I noticed a majestic, cute-looking white husky,
And I petted it. All I did was play with the cute white husky.

After a minute, as I was still playing with the cute white husky,
I started feeling drowsy and heavy-eyed, and it seemed blurry in my eyes,
As I looked around the brown wood from the treehouse,
It started to look like a wardrobe,
Even the cute white husky started to look like a pillow...

I started to move slowly and I made a big, giant, lethargic dopey yawn,
"I feel dizzy," I said and found myself in my bedroom,
"Oh well... it was just a dream," I said.

Oluwadara Kehinde (9)
The Free School Norwich, Norwich

The Swirl Twirl

Swirl, twirl, I feel like I am starting to dance,
I had competitions, feeling like something momentarily would happen!
Oh no, oh no, oh no!
As everyone's eyes were flabbergasted
When they looked at me!

Swirl, twirl, as the music started to play,
I kept dancing and prancing!
My feet were exhausted and tired.
Oh no, oh, no, oh no!
It's like I can't control my feet anymore.

Swirl, twirl, I heard a high-pitched sound come next to me,
I jumped up and saw my hard, white rocking chair
And my cuddly, adorable toys!
But I realised it was a dream,
But I had to go to school,
Oh no, oh no, oh no!

Xenia Cotruta (9)
The Free School Norwich, Norwich

I Was Chased By A Hooded Figure

I was chased by a hooded figure.
It was dark as night.
I was running in fright; so dark, like space.
He was mythical, so majestic, it almost made me shiver.
I hurt myself, ouch!

I was chased by a hooded figure.
He was fading away.
I could see the trees fading as I ran.
I could hear someone moving, who could that be?
Everything was fading in a blink of an eye.

I was chased by a hooded figure.
I opened my eyes.
It turned out it was a dream and I was sleepwalking.
That's how I got hurt, oh.
Now I know, it was just a nightmare.
He he he...
I wonder, how did I get up to the haunted stairs?

Phong Nguyen (8)
The Free School Norwich, Norwich

Falling From The Sky

I remember,
Frantically falling from a tall building.
At that moment, I looked up,
I saw somebody!
I moved my hands deliberately as if they were wings.
Suddenly, they turned into wings!
As I shook my head in happiness, I caught a glimpse of him,
He was flying!

I remember,
The person looked like my teddy.
The building looked like my closet,
Then I asked, "But wait! Somebody pinch me!"

I remember,
My alarm went off.
I got up to see my teddy, which was right smack on top of me!
I saw my closet, which looked like the building,
Then I finally realised it was all a dream.

Advay Jain (8)
The Free School Norwich, Norwich

A Kidnapped Dream

I was tied to a chair,
It was pitch-black dark,
Nothing to see but a light of flee,
I untied myself from the chair,
I bounded over the electrical fence,
I saw my spinosaurus and a dragon,
Then the gates opened.

I was tied to a chair,
There was an army of...
Cats! I commanded an attack,
There were cats on the ground,
Then I escaped the cats,
Then I thought,
Why is there a white, fluffy dragon on me?
The sun is on a metal pole.

I was outside the building,
It was pitch-black for a second,
I saw my bedroom furniture,
Then I realised that it was just a dream.

Ashish Madarapu (9)
The Free School Norwich, Norwich

The Day I Was In A Dream

I once was in a dream.
I once was in a city all alone.
No people, no shops open, just me.
The houses were flooded and fell apart
In one single raindrop.

I once was in a dream.
But then, some houses looked familiar.
I felt a little sad all alone,
But this floor felt a little soft and fluffy.
That door had big golden door handles; weird.

I once was in a dream.
I started to feel strange.
I said, "Someone pinch me,"
Then I felt my mouth move.
Suddenly, that big bell started to ring
And sounded like my alarm,
I woke up,
And realised...
It was all a dream.

Alfie Reid (8)
The Free School Norwich, Norwich

Vampirina

I was Vampirina in Transylvania,
There were monsters everywhere
And I loved it!
I saw all of Vampirina's friends,
They waved at me,
But hardly spoke a word.
And I saw Vampirina's parents.

I was Vampirina,
Everything was like everything from my bedroom.
I was half awake,
The floor felt like my bed,
It turned all pink,
Like my doorway,
And I saw the sun rising.

I heard an alarm, beep, beep, beep!
I realised it was the dream
I have every day,
And I saw my mum,
She brought me breakfast in bed.
It was my favourite!
I got dressed.

Skye Bramley (9)
The Free School Norwich, Norwich

The Tunnel

I am in a tunnel,
A dark, dark tunnel,
I walk through the damp underpass,
But then it shuts,
I turn on my flashlight,
And I walk, walk, walk,
I smell rats and squirrels,
I taste the dirty air,
I see nothing just black,
I hear the squeaks of rats fading...

I am in a tunnel,
But the floor is falling,
I scream loudly,
I hear screams, other screams,
I see something - it looks like my bed,
I see something - it looks like my desk,
I see something - it looks like my...
Mum's making breakfast,
Then I close my eyes...

Evelyn Smithson (9)
The Free School Norwich, Norwich

Enchanted Forest

Footprints, wind whispering,
I was in an enchanted forest,
There were footprints in the mud.
I felt something pushing me,
I fell to the ground.
What was that noise?

A bunny popped out; it flopped its ears.
It was telling me to follow it.
The bunny led me to a cave.

In the cave, there were crystals and healing water.
When I jumped into the water,
I thought, *wait, that's my Bunny-Hops, my best teddy.*

In a flash, I started to drown!
I heard someone shouting my name, "Wake up!"
It was a dream!

Bella Atkinson-Neill (9)
The Free School Norwich, Norwich

In A Desert

I am in a desert.
Walking to a dig site.
I have a brush, chisel and hammer.
I am ready.
I am at the dig site and I have found a bone.

I am in a desert.
And I have found a bone.
But wait, is it just me?
That looks particularly like a cuddly.
The sand feels like a duvet, how strange.

I am in a desert.
But it's swaying, how strange.
Someone's pinched me, ow, that hurt.
I open my eyes, it can't be true.
It was just a dream.

Sam Emmins (9)
The Free School Norwich, Norwich

I Remember

Someone chasing me at midnight,
I was scared,
Because there was no light,
They pushed me into a dark room,
I heard footsteps and strange sounds,
Unable to move he trapped me,
Handcuffed in a dark room, worried,
What happened to me, why me?
I saw something not very pleasant,
I saw a skeleton with blood...

I remember...

Someone was tapping me on the shoulder,
They were calling my name,
It was a person,
Not tall, not small but medium.

Lyla Hawes (9)
The Free School Norwich, Norwich

Fortnite Buddies

We're jumping off the battle bus,
In Fortnite, Alfie screamed!
They no-scoped one for me,
Killed a player from 1,000 metres away.

Online, I hit the target,
Oh no! We dropped all our medallions,
I picked them up,
And got the last player.

Suddenly, my alarm rang,
And I woke up,
It was just a dream,
I was back in the lobby,
With Alfie, Isaac and Rufus too!
We played red vs blue,
This time for real...

Lee Codling (9)
The Free School Norwich, Norwich

Dreams

I was Taylor Swift
My knees trembled
As I walked on stage
I was so nervous
But then everybody
Started cheering
Then I was happy

I was Taylor Swift
I was so happy
When I saw
All of my fans
They shouted my name
I felt like a superstar
Shiny bright and flying

Suddenly I felt
Something pinching me
Then I saw
My bed and my table
Then my alarm went off
Then it was all a dream.

Willow Davison (8)
The Free School Norwich, Norwich

Untitled

Oh, little girl, beware, beware,
Oh, little girl, the monster is there.
Oh, little girl, beware, beware,
Oh, little girl, the monster is there.
In the deep, dark woods,
They're off on a stroll.

Then, out of nowhere,
Came a one-eyed Face-Fader,
A horrible beast from the shadows.
If you show any emotion
It will steal your face!

Oh, little girl, beware, beware,
Oh, little girl, the monster is there!

Amelie Airgibi (9)
The Free School Norwich, Norwich

Untitled

I was in a field?
Cows grazing on the flowering grass.
Pairs of ferrets, running through the ferns.
Small oak trees surrounding one mighty oak.

I bent down and touched the grass.
And it started to feel like my bed sheet?
Then I looked up, and saw a rocking horse?
Startled, I closed my eyes and opened them again.

And… I was in my bed?!
It was a dream? Huh?
At least it was a good one.
Not a bad one.

Yolandi-Joan Reynolds (8)
The Free School Norwich, Norwich

Dancing

I am putting on tap shoes on the stage,
I am practising lots of my skills.
I am sitting in the changing room,
Waiting to go and dance.
Just then, I am jumping and galloping.

Suddenly, I feel my glowing stick!
The more I feel it, the more it feels real.
When I get on stage,
It feels like I am sleepwalking on the edge of the stage!

I am awake in the kitchen,
It was just a dream,
But it felt real.

Samuel Allen (8)
The Free School Norwich, Norwich

I Am A Gladiator

I am a gladiator,
Fighting in the lightning,
The crowd cheers,
I feel pressure,
The most pressure in the world.

Bradley Walsh is on a poster for a minute,
Why am I flashing?
A wardrobe - what?
Is it real?
Do I know?
Do you know?
Who knows?

I am a gladiator,
Yes or no?
A ding, ding, ding sound,
What is going on?
I feel disorientated.
It was a dream.

Rufus Rix (8)
The Free School Norwich, Norwich

Fortnite

Isaac was in his house,
He was playing Fortnite,
And he was cranking 90s!

Until the pro gamer, Isaac got low on health
And he had no heals!
But his team got them,
Until one looked like his brother.

I felt some pushing and pulling,
Also some ringing
And I noticed it was all a dream...

Isaac Butler (8)
The Free School Norwich, Norwich

Wizards Of Once

Out in the forest, not far away,
Me and the wizards come out to play.
One has a dragon, one has a bear,
One has a snow leopard, with no hair!
The wizards are dragons, the wizards are kind,
One is intelligent and can read minds.
You can come to play,
We will stay up all day,
Come on down,
Come have fun,
For we are the wizards,
The Wizards of Once.
If you annoy Xar, he will get angry,
But Bodkin the bodyguard is very hangry.
Queen Sychorax is mean and very stubborn,
She killed a witch who landed on her bottom!
Squeeze Joos sacrificed himself,
And all the others cried,
Will he survive, or will he die?
Crusher, the giant, has a very kind soul,
But the warriors captured him and took him to a stone,
A stone that took away magic powers,
That leaves the prisoners crying for hours and hours.

They're very nice, they won't fright,
And they don't like a fight,
So nice to meet you, it was fun,
Thanks for meeting, the Wizards of Once.

Ellie Clamp (10)
The Woodlands Community Primary School, Glascote

What I See

The world is big and round,
There are loads of people on the ground.
We don't hear a peep when everyone is asleep,
Unless a mouse goes squeak!

I look outside and what can I see?
Big, tall trees with green leaves
And beautiful flowers that are staring at me.
The sun is shining down on me,
Every time I look at it, I can't see.

In the winter I look outside, what can I see?
I see frosted cars all around me.
When it snows and becomes icy,
People ice skating and sledging around me.

In the autumn I look outside, what can I see?
The leaves change their colour day by day.
They are very pretty, they mound up on people's drives
Which drives my daddy crazy, he sweeps them off daily.

In the spring I look outside, what can I see?
Rabbits jumping around like the Easter bunny.
Bees collecting the pollen to make honey,
Writing this poem is making me hungry.

Leila Morrissey (7)
The Woodlands Community Primary School, Glascote

The Dance Of Life

D ance away milady, take the dance floor with you,
A nyone would want to dance like you, flowing left and right,
N obody can dance like you, so dance away milady, dance away,
C ome and dance the night away, now and forever,
E veryone's eyes are on you, so dance away milady.

O ut of everyone, you are the prettiest dancer, so dance, dance, dance,
F or to love those feet is to dance and dance away.

L illy is her name, and she dances and dances every night,
I n the dance party, I love you,
F inally, the night has ended, so no more dancing tonight,
E ven though the night has ended, you're still dancing away, with no care in the world.

As you walk home,
Your head is still swaying to the music,
So dance away,
Her best friend is,
Alexi-Grace and she helps her.

Betsy Whiston (10)
The Woodlands Community Primary School, Glascote

A Magical Land

This isn't a dream,
About how to fly.
This isn't a dream,
About how to pass by like a spy.
This is a dream,
About a little girl's fantasies.
Amelia is very familiar with her magical land,
She dreams of it, night and day.
In Amelia's magical land,
She dreams of peace and love,
With harmony to which we all stand.
In the magical land,
Trees stand and sway,
The emerald, glittering grass,
Is there for all to lay.
No one can see better than others,
We are all united as brothers.
In the magical land,
Children can stay up all night and day,
And no rules to make us pay.
In the magical land,
We all work together,
Like the sun and moon,

Which helps light up the day.
Until the magic land becomes a reality,
Let's all love and care,
And let's be fair.

Amelia Sleet (10)
The Woodlands Community Primary School, Glascote

Danger Of The Sea

There once was a boat that went out to sea,
But the person who was steering it didn't know,
About the dangers of the sea.

The waves are that big,
They have covered a city,
Just imagine your whole life,
Has been taken away with one sweep.

There is so much pollution and chemicals,
In the sea,
It's killing the mammals,
That you cannot see.

These mammals can swim,
Deep in the sea,
It is 35,000 feet at challenger deep.

There are thirty-two mammals,
That are a danger in the sea,
Can you name them with me?
There are lionfish, jellyfish, sea snails,
I wouldn't like them near me,
Would you?

There are 236,000 deaths in the sea,
So just remember how dangerous it can be.

Jacob Morrissey (10)
The Woodlands Community Primary School, Glascote

Winding World

I'm trapped inside a clock,
Tick-tock, tick-tock,
Oh no! I need to get out before it strikes 8 o'clock,
The only things I can see are objects turning,
Every step I take feels like it's burning,
Look forwards in the middle!
A riddle!
To get closer to the answer,
You need to get closer to the time,
That's it!
If you get closer to the time,
You need to get closer to where the clock chimes,
So it's where the clock's hands are,
The front bit of the clock,
Tick-tock, tick-tock,
There it goes again, I really need to hurry up,
Look, a light!
But the pathway is really tight,
I'm never going to get through there,
Unless,
Look, a strand of rope,
Well, I'm guessing this is my only hope.

Sienna Nika (9)
The Woodlands Community Primary School, Glascote

Me And My Teddies!

Bang, thunder there, *bang*, thunder here,
In my head I am thinking, *why am I here?*
"Aargh," I said, I thought I was dead,
My other teddy was quite near.

I felt a shiver from head to toe,
I saw my deer, sooo,
What is happening?
All night long, I thought I was there,
My door was opening, while I was brushing my hair.

One not there and one not here,
When I was done, I looked over my bed...
It was Bo, he was holding the Nerf gun,
I told him off, I grabbed him and put him to bed.

The moth was attracted to the light,
My teddy is called Ted,
It is a bear,
The thunder strikes again, *bang!*
I woke up again and I had a good rest.

Iyla Ford (10)
The Woodlands Community Primary School, Glascote

Dreamy Dragons

There once were two brave dragons
Who flew without a care,
They went to many places,
That others wouldn't dare.
Over forbidden mountains,
Down into deep dark lakes,
They just loved adventure,
And would do whatever it takes.
One day, they went into a cave
And found a princess there,
Trapped by an ogre,
Deep inside his lair.
How could they free her,
They thought of just the plan,
One would distract the ogre
While the princess and the other ran.
The king was so grateful
That the princess was home at last
He wanted to reward them
So a new law was passed.
The dragons would be free to roam
Without any trouble or hassle

And when they grew too old to fly
They could live inside the castle.

Margot Clark Macnab (7)
The Woodlands Community Primary School, Glascote

My Friend, Yeti

I had an adventurous dream,
When I was sailing down a big, frozen stream,
I came across a yeti,
Who was eating spaghetti,
In a land of ice and snow, so white,
Lived the yeti, big and bright,
With fur as soft as fluffy clouds,
He roams the mountains,
My new friend Yeti really makes me proud,
His footsteps leave a trail of joy,
As he plays with polar bears, oh boy!
His laughter echoes through the icy peaks,
Tickling penguins and playing hide-and-seek,
He sleeps in a crystal cave,
If you enter you must behave,
But don't be scared little one,
The yeti's heart is warm, full of fun,
So if you visit this snowy height,
You might just meet my friend, Yeti, gleaming white.

Evelae Amiss (8)
The Woodlands Community Primary School, Glascote

Infinity Island

On my walk, I see some trees,
And, of course, some busy bees.
I'm not expecting anything nice,
There could be an eagle or maybe woodlice!

I come to a lovely park,
And suddenly, it gives me a spark.
Treasure Island, just across the moat,
About to wet my feet, I spy a little boat.

My first shaking, muddy step on the island's shore,
Something moves the undergrowth; I'm scared to my core.
Maybe the stories that they tell about this place are true,
I stop, I shriek, what am I going to do?

The sun breaks through and lights the way,
A bunny hops out as if to say,
The busy bees in the trees so tall,
Aren't so bad after all.

Bethany Milligan (7)
The Woodlands Community Primary School, Glascote

My Teddy Had A Nightmare

I woke up, it smelt weird.
Like something that was in smoke.
There was a teddy and it was dark all of a sudden.
The teddy's name was Ted Small,
It was walking here.
Then the teddy called me
And all the lights flickered; *boom!*
I heard a voice.
It asked me, "Do you see the moon?"
It was late but they looked happy meeting me,
But I was looking at the stars,
They were hovering to make shapes,
First, there was a jellyfish, then a stingray, which stung someone,
A mammoth, then a mountain.
It was quite long but I don't know the name,
I fell asleep,
It was the creepiest night ever.

Lily-Ann Woolley (7)
The Woodlands Community Primary School, Glascote

Fairy Friends

F airies that are friends, oh fairies that are friends,
A t night, they come out to play,
I t's the best time all day,
R uby is one of my fairy friends,
Y es! It's night again.

F airies that are friends, oh fairies that are friends,
R eady to play, ready to tag,
I 'm here, I'm here, oh, I'm late,
E ven though it's a rainy day, they still come to play,
N ight ends and I am sad, but I still had fairy fun,
D ance is what we do when we are not playing tag,
S ometimes I play with Kara and Ellie, my fairy friends.

Alexi-Grace Jones (10)
The Woodlands Community Primary School, Glascote

Nightmares

N othing is the same as I normally see,
I t is all strange, weird and mysterious,
G oing on into the darkness and it feels like I'm going nowhere,
H ours waiting, doing the same thing and it just makes it worse,
T hud! I see something coming towards me,
M y worst fear is clowns and spiders everywhere!
A nything else? I think, *will anyone save me?*
R escue me please, anything to get me away from it and then I can see,
E veryone! It's my friends and family, they have come to rescue me,
S uddenly, I find myself in bed and I finally get away.

Laura Merrall (7)
The Woodlands Community Primary School, Glascote

Solar And Lunar Eclipse

The light of the sun,
Oh so bright,
The reflection of the moon,
Through the night,
When they collide,
It makes a sight,
But to see it,
It might take a flight,
When the moon covers the sun,
It's a solar eclipse,
When the moon's in the Earth's shadow,
It's a lunar eclipse,
A reddish colour,
The moon may take,
A fabulous sight it will make,
Without the light,
It still sticks out from the stars,
It's redder than Mars,
When the moon's in the Earth's way,
It's a lunar eclipse,
When the moon covers the sun,
It's a solar eclipse.

Sid Chester (10)
The Woodlands Community Primary School, Glascote

Golden Bay

Golden Bay
I quickly swam away
In the icy blue
I finally saw you
A picture in my head
I can finally go to bed
But the adventure doesn't end yet
You'll see and you'll bet
For in the dark holds an ark
For some fairy tales to tell
Rang the grand yard bell
There was a home for the gnome
And a house for the mouse
There should be some pixie dust
Between the fairies, there is trust
When I left this magical land
I shook a fairy's hand
It was very clear
That I shouldn't fear
So I formed a happy tear.

Ella Jarratt (8)
The Woodlands Community Primary School, Glascote

Nightmares

N othing scares me more than the dark.
I n the dark, I fear the worst.
G laring at the moon gives me the creeps.
H oping one day this feeling will go away.
T rees swaying from side to side in the moonlight.
M idnight comes to start a new day.
A wake, I become, and my nightmares disappear.
R eady for the day, I jump out of bed.
E xhausted after my terrible dreams,
S adly, the night will return.

Lucy-Mae Goodfellow (10)
The Woodlands Community Primary School, Glascote

A Football Star

The greatest footballer of all time is me,
Enchantingly scoring a goal,
Like the world has never seen before,
Strong, but quite frantically kicking a ball,
As high as a rocket in outer space,
Speaking about rockets,
It was as fast as a rocket going up to outer space,
Some people's fantasy, says he is not the best,
But their brain was a mess,
His shots are good,
But it needs to flood,
His shots are frightening,
As a monster biting.

Isaac Sulka (8)
The Woodlands Community Primary School, Glascote

Dragon Dreams

In my dreams every night,
I get to see a wonderful sight,
Me and my dragon flying high,
Soaring through the bright lit sky.

Shooting stars up above,
All of which I really love,
The moon full and bright,
Lets off an illuminating light,
If I'm lucky, I will see,
Some colourful lights across the sea.

Isabel Poll (9)
The Woodlands Community Primary School, Glascote

Teddies

My teddies were sleeping,
When I heard a noise, *bang! Smash!*
I jumped out of my bed,
And I looked out of my window,
And there was nothing,
So I went downstairs to get my water,
And there was nothing there,
So I went back to my bed,
And my teddies gave me a hug,
And I went to sleep with them.

Poppie Jackson (9)
The Woodlands Community Primary School, Glascote

The Dog Who Has The Gift

My magical Bella
Grants me wishes
With a cute patch of fur
On her head no one misses
I kiss for good luck
And a wish to come true
She gifts it to me
With a whisper from me to you
I feel so lucky
And grateful it's true
Her patch of magic
And the love we share too.

Harriet Nicholls (8)
The Woodlands Community Primary School, Glascote

Lights In The Night

Starlight, star bright,
I see you every night,
You and your mates,
The shapes that you make,
Dancing in the night,
Elegant and bright,
Different sizes, different lights,
Will I see you tomorrow night?

Oscar Wakelin (10)
The Woodlands Community Primary School, Glascote

Swimming With Dolphins

Every day I wonder,
Was that a dream?
Swimming with dolphins,
But not in a stream.
It takes place in the ocean,
And going on a boat,
But when it comes to finding them,
It's not as easy as you thought.
So I looked in the sea,
And thought with a wonder,
Where on earth could they be?
Then I saw a splash and a fin and a blast,
Then I could see a beautiful dolphin,
Swimming close to me,
As the people got into the water,
The excitement flew fast,
So I jumped into the water,
With a right big splash.
I felt like I was sitting on something,
Something silky and blue,
When I looked at it,
I knew it was true!

Isabella Castle (9)
Whalley CE Primary School, Whalley

The Jungle Chase

Once upon a night-time dream,
In a magical forest,
Was a dragon-riding team.

Ben, Pip and Alex slalomed through the trees,
Being chased,
By half-teachers, half-monsters,
"Help, please!"

Adrenaline rushed as we hopped on our dragons,
They were,
Much better than cars, planes or wagons.

Twisting and darting and turning the turns,
Avoiding the bark,
Which can give you burns.

Leaves swirled as the monster drew near,
Dragons scared,
Me too, tensing with fear.

"Roar!" went my dragon,
Who turned and breathed flame,
Shrieking, the monsters fell down,
Putting them to shame.

Soaring the landscape of a broad mass of plants,
We landed by a castle,
A unicorn guarding, horn sharp as a lance.

Grey brick and stone,
Surrounded us all,
As we went,
Through a door in a wall.

All of our animal friends were here, all safe,
I then chanted a spell,
"Kanwoobi katarase!"

Boom! We blasted off into space,
Click! I was back in bed,
My room is just the same,
Wow! I wish I could have this dream again.

Benjamin Allen (10)
Whalley CE Primary School, Whalley

Fast Food!

I open the front door with a bang,
And walk straight into the kitchen,
I open the fridge door,
With my mouth wide open.

Everything in the fridge is gone,
And my family are not home,
I turn my head around,
I see them!

All the food in the fridge has escaped,
And they are running around wildly,
I don't know what to do,
They are standing right beside me.

I call them over to the fridge,
They come running over at the speed of light,
I close the fridge door,
Wow, they are fast food!

Harriet Parkin (9)
Whalley CE Primary School, Whalley

I Had A Dream

I had a dream that I could fly,
High up in the sky,
Oh, I had a dream,
About clowns running around,
They all frowned.

I had a dream,
About fairies,
Who give you only one glance,
Before they disappear,
Because you only see them,
Once a year,
I had a dream.

Sapphire Webster (10)
Whalley CE Primary School, Whalley

One Wonderful Dream

I had a dream,
when I was with a team.
We went to a waterfall,
to do a trust fall.
I had a great time,
until I saw a mime.
It was a great day,
but I had to pay.

Danielle Bassett (10)
Whalley CE Primary School, Whalley

YOUNG WRITERS INFORMATION

We hope you have enjoyed reading this book – and that you will continue to in the coming years.

If you're a young writer who enjoys reading and creative writing, or the parent of an enthusiastic poet or story writer, do visit our website www.youngwriters.co.uk. Here you will find free competitions, workshops and games, as well as recommended reads, a poetry glossary and our blog.

If you would like to order further copies of this book, or any of our other titles, then please give us a call or visit www.youngwriters.co.uk.

Young Writers
Remus House
Coltsfoot Drive
Peterborough
PE2 9BF
(01733) 890066
info@youngwriters.co.uk

YoungWritersUK YoungWritersCW
youngwriterscw youngwriterscw